A NOTE TO PARENTS

When your children are ready to "step into reading," giving them the right books—and lots of them—is as crucial as giving them the right food to eat. **Step into Reading Books** present exciting stories or information reinforced with lively, colorful illustrations that make learning to read fun, satisfying, and worthwhile. They are priced so that acquiring an entire library of them is affordable. And they are beginning readers with an important difference—they're written on three levels.

Step 1 Books, with their very large type and extremely simple vocabulary, have been created for the very youngest readers. **Step 2 Books** are both longer and slightly more difficult. **Step 3 Books,** written to mid-second-grade reading levels, are for the child who has acquired even greater reading skills.

Children develop at different ages. **Step into Reading Books,** with their three levels of reading, are designed to help children become good—and interested—readers *faster.* The grade levels assigned to the three steps—preschool through grade 1 for Step 1, grades 1 through 3 for Step 2, and grades 2 and 3 for Step 3—are intended only as guides. Some children move through all three steps very rapidly; others climb the steps over a period of several years. These books will help your child "step into reading" in style!

Text copyright © 1986 by Dorothy F. Haas. Illustrations copyright © 1986 by C. S. Ewing. All rights reserved under International and Pan-American Copyright Conventions. Published in the United States by Random House, Inc., New York, and simultaneously in Canada by Random House of Canada Limited, Toronto.

Library of Congress Cataloging-in-Publication Data: Haas, Dorothy F. Dorothy and old King Crow. (Step into reading. A Step 3 book) SUMMARY: Luckily for Dorothy, Spelling Bee helps her spell a hard word so she can break King Crow's spell over Scarecrow. [1. English language—Spelling—Fiction] I. Ewing, C. S., ill. II. Title. III. Series: Step into reading. Step 3 book. PZ7.H1124Dm 1986 [E] 86-3824 ISBN: 0-394-88227-X (trade); 0-394-98227-4 (lib. bdg.)

Manufactured in the United States of America 1 2 3 4 5 6 7 8 9 0

STEP INTO READING is a trademark of Random House, Inc.

Step into Reading

Dorothy and Old King Crow

by Dorothy Haas
illustrated by C.S. Ewing

A Step 3 Book

Random House 🏠 New York

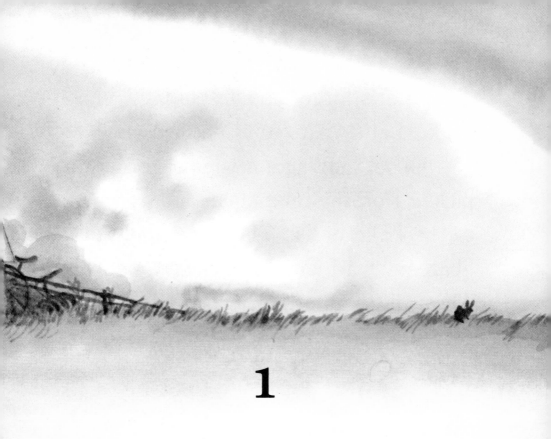

1

One day Dorothy came home from school. Her dog, Toto, ran to meet her. She picked him up and he barked.

"Are you asking what I did in school today?" she asked. She sighed. "I was the first one to go down in our spelling bee. I spelled balloon with one l."

Dorothy looked sad. Toto licked her chin.

"Let's forget about spelling," she said. "Let's visit our friends in Oz."

Once, long ago, a windy storm picked Dorothy up and carried her away to the Land of Oz. There she met a Scarecrow, a Lion, and a Tin Woodman. They all became the best of friends.

Together they visited the Wizard of Oz. The Wizard gave brains to the Scarecrow. He gave courage to the Lion. And he gave a heart to the Tin Woodman.

After that Dorothy was able to go back to Oz whenever she liked.

Now she took her magic handkerchief out of her pocket. She waved it. And just like that she was back in Oz!

There stood her friends—the Lion, the Scarecrow, and the Tin Woodman.

"Little Dorothy!" said the Lion.

"Come to visit!" said the Tin Woodman.

"We will have a wonderful time!" said the Scarecrow. "We can visit Princess Ozma!"

"But not until tomorrow," said the Lion. "It's getting dark."

"We will need a fire," said the Tin Woodman. "I will find some wood."

"We will need water, too," said the Lion. "I will look for a stream."

"You will need some supper, Dorothy," said the Scarecrow. "I will find some berries for you."

And away they went.

2

The Tin Woodman did not go far before he found some dry sticks. He carried them back to Dorothy.

The Lion found a clear stream. He took a good long drink. Then he carried some water back to Dorothy.

The Scarecrow walked for a long time. Then he saw a bush. It was covered with red berries.

"Just the thing!" he said.

He took off his hat. He began to fill it with berries.

"Swish-sh-shhhhh."

What was that?

The Scarecrow looked around.

He did not see anybody.

But he did see another bush. It was covered with blueberries.

"If I could eat," he said, "I would like some of these."

He began picking the blueberries.

"Swish-sh-sh-shhhh..."

The noise was louder.
Shadows moved in the trees.
"Is anybody there?" called the
Scarecrow.
Nobody answered.

"It must be the wind moving the leaves," thought the Scarecrow.

Then he saw some blackberries. "They look good," he said. "I will just take a few of those."

"SWISH-SH-SH-SHHHHHHH."

Dark shadows flew out of the trees. They swooped down on the Scarecrow.

"Oh, no!" he cried. "No. Help!"

3

The forest got darker and darker.

"Where can the Scarecrow be?" wondered Dorothy.

"He will come soon," said the Tin Woodman.

But the Scarecrow did not return.

Dorothy called to him.

The Lion roared.

The Tin Woodman banged on his tin leg.

But the Scarecrow did not answer.

"What if something terrible has happened to him?" said Dorothy.

"Don't be afraid," said the Tin Woodman. "We will find our friend."

And they went looking for the Scarecrow. They searched all night long. But they did not find him.

When the sun came up they found something else—the Scarecrow's hat.

"And look there!" said the Tin Woodman. He pointed. "Straw!"

"Why, that must be the Scarecrow's stuffing," said Dorothy.

Farther along they found more straw. And after that they found still more.

"I do believe the Scarecrow left a trail of straw for us," said Dorothy.

"He knew we would hunt for him," said the Tin Woodman.

"But where can he be?" asked the Lion.

None of them could guess.

They went along, following the trail of straw.

Suddenly Toto barked.

"I think Toto hears something," said Dorothy.

They stopped and listened.

Was somebody singing?

Toto ran ahead of them.

Dorothy and the others followed.

They pushed through bushes.

They went around a big rock.

And there was the Scarecrow. He was singing:

"Crows are nice.
Crows are good.
I love crows,
And everyone should."

"Dear Scarecrow," said Dorothy. "I am so glad we found you! Where have you been?"

The Scarecrow looked at her. But he did not answer. He just went on singing.

"Never, never, never
Will I ever, ever, ever
Scare another crow."

Dorothy sat back on her heels. "Something is wrong!" she wailed.

Some crows were sitting in a tree.
"Caw!" they called. "Caw!"

"Goodness knows,
    I love crows,"

sang the Scarecrow.
    "Caw-haw!" laughed the crows.
"Caw-haw-haw-haw!"

"Scarecrow does not love crows," said the Tin Woodman.

"He is under a magic spell," said the Lion.

"And it's not true about crows being good," said Dorothy. "Crows are bad!"

"Girl!" said a loud voice. "You are unkind to us!"

4

Dorothy looked up.

Sitting in a tree was a large crow with a crown on his head.

"We are jolly good fellows," he said.

"You carried away my friend the Scarecrow!" said Dorothy.

"True," said King Crow. "My crows did bring him to me."

"But why?" asked Dorothy.

"Scarecrows always try to scare us," said King Crow. "So we gave your friend a good scare. He kept calling 'Help! Help!' Oh, it was all very jolly!"

He laughed.

"Caw-haw-haw," laughed the other crows.

"That is not one bit jolly," said Dorothy. "And it was not jolly to put a spell on the Scarecrow, either. Now he even thinks you are nice!"

"And so we are," said King Crow.

"You are a big bully," said Dorothy.

She turned to the Lion and the
Tin Woodman. "I cannot help the
Scarecrow," she said sadly. "The only
kind of spell I know is the kind we do in
school—spelling. And I'm a terrible
speller. I always lose in spelling bees."

"Girl!" called King Crow. "I will
show you that I am a jolly good fellow. I
will say a word. If you can spell the
word, the magic spell will be broken."

Dorothy did not say anything. Spell something? How could she?

"I will make it easy for you," said King Crow. "I will say it slowly. Bam... boo...zle...ment."

"Bam—WHAT?" asked Dorothy.

King Crow said the word again. "I will come back in one hour," he said. "If you can spell that word, the Scarecrow can go free."

He laughed. "But you will not be able to spell it, of course."

Then he flew away. The other crows flew with him. "Caw-haw-haw," they called.

"Let's give a cheer
    for good King Crow,"

sang the Scarecrow.

"He's the smartest
    crow I know."

Dorothy sat on a log. "Poor Scarecrow," she said. "He will never be free. That big word is much too hard for me to spell."

5

Someone spoke. "It might be hard for you. But it is easy for me."

Dorothy looked up. A bee was flying around a sunflower.

"Spelling Bee is my name," said the bee. "And I have come to your rescue. R-e-s-c-u-e. I can spell anything."

"You mean you will help me?" asked Dorothy.

"Gladly," said the Spelling Bee. "Old King Crow needs a lesson!"

Then she told Dorothy how to spell "bamboozlement." She made her spell it ten times.

"What a funny word!" said Dorothy. "What does it mean?"

"It means a trick," said the Spelling Bee. "King Crow is playing a trick on you. He thinks you cannot spell 'bamboozlement.' But now he is going to learn a thing or two about tricks."

Dorothy smiled. She sat down to wait. Toto, the Lion, and the Tin Woodman sat down beside her.

Soon King Crow came back.

"Well, girl," he called. "Spell the word—if you can."

"B-a-m," Dorothy said slowly.

"Ha!" said King Crow. "That is the easy part. You cannot do it."

"—b-o-o," Dorothy went on.

"Caw-caw-caw," called the crows. They flew around Dorothy's head.

"—z-l-e," said Dorothy.

King Crow began to look unhappy.

"—m-e-n-t," said Dorothy.

"Very good!" said the Spelling Bee.

"NO!" screeched King Crow. He glared at the Spelling Bee. "I have been tricked!"

"Yes," said Dorothy. She spelled the word again very fast.

"B-a-m-b-o-o-z-l-e-m-e-n-t."

With that, the Scarecrow shook his head. He looked around. "Why, hello, my friends," he said.

"Caw!" cried the crows. "The Scarecrow is awake! Caw!"

They flew to the top of a tree. "Swish-sh-sh."

"Girl!" screamed King Crow. "You said you were a terrible speller. I heard you. That was the hardest word I know. You tricked me! The Spelling Bee helped you. No fair!"

He threw his crown on the ground. He hopped up and down and flapped his wings.

"You were not fair," said Dorothy. "You tried to trick me. But your old bamboozlement did not work. And now we have our friend back."

She hugged the Scarecrow.

He sat up and scratched his head.

"Now I remember what happened," he said. He looked at the crows up in the tree. "When I was not looking those crows picked me up. They carried me here—to him." He pointed at King Crow.

"Bamboozled!" said King Crow. "Me! King Crow!" He looked very cross.

"King," called the Scarecrow. "I am sorry to tell you this. You have no brains. If you did, you would know better than to try to trick Dorothy."

"Brains," said the Spelling Bee. "B-r-a-i-n-s."

"King," called the Lion, "your crows jumped on our friend when he was not looking. None of you has any courage."

"Courage," said the Spelling Bee. "C-o-u-r-a-g-e."

"King!" called the Tin Woodman. "You have no heart. If you had a heart, you would try to be kinder."

"Heart," said the Spelling Bee. "H-e-a-r-t."

"If you like," called Dorothy, "you can come with us to visit Princess Ozma. She will give you brains and courage and a heart."

"Humph!" said King Crow. "I am fine just the way I am. I am a jolly good fellow."

But he did not look jolly. He looked grumpy. "Bamboozled," he said again. "By a little girl!"

"And by me," said the Spelling Bee. "S-p-e-l-l-i-n-g B-e-e."

Everyone laughed. Dorothy laughed hardest of all. She pulled out her handkerchief to wipe her eyes.

The handkerchief gave a little wave.
In a wink Dorothy was back home.

"Oh, Toto," she said. "I did not
mean to come home so soon."

Then she remembered King Crow
and laughed again. "Do you suppose he
will always be grumpy? G-r-u-m-p-y.
Even I can spell that!"